Matilda's Mischief

This Book Belongs to

Dedication

To she of equal Mischief

And my sister whom without this would not be possible

First Published 2022

Text © James Pluckrose

Characters and Illustrations © James Pluckrose

Editing by ZP.Inc

ISBN – 9798370028335 –

Other books by James Pluckrose

Alice Anderson - A Mountain Walk

Matilda's Mischief - Medieval meddling

Nanny's Silver Box

6

Extreme Fishing

43

Little Garden Helpers

Helpers 79

Medieval Meddling

103

Nanny's Silver Box

It was Saturday and after a busy week at school, Matilda, more commonly known by her friends as Tilly would normally sleep in. However instead today was going to be a very important day, it was her Nanny's 70th birthday  and Mum and Dad were setting up for a big family BBQ.

 She started her day by brushing out her hair and wrapped a ribbon to create her signature ponytail. After that, Tilly was already to go. Her two best friends had been invited around as their parents were also helping Tilly's parents. There

was a collection of siblings, aunts, uncles, brothers, sisters, friends and neighbours all invited to this special occasion. It was going to be a very busy day!

After following her taste for toast, a quick breakfast, Tilly pulled out her roller skates from under the dining table and called out into the garden. "Mum, can we go across to the park for a bit?" she asked.

"Yes, but we're going to have an early lunch, everyone's arriving about one o'clock and I would like you girls to be there!" Called Tilly's mum.

"We will!" Tilly shouted as she ran back in to the living room where a collection of siblings were watching the television and making their way through breakfast. "Amelia, Harley, you both want to come?" she asked.

The two girls jumped from the group excitedly. These three girls are the best of friends, they all live on the same street, go to the same school and are all in the same class. They love doing everything together.

Luckily there is a very nice field and park right across the street from their houses so the girls have a great space to play. As Tilly began to lock on her roller skates, Harley grabbed her scooter and Amelia kicked her skateboard and caught it with her prosthetic left hand.

On Amelia's left arm from her elbow down is finely designed and intelligent construction of composite  components which act and work like a real arm,

"Are we're ready to roll girls?" Amelia asked excitedly.

The three girls raced out of the house, spending time running and riding around the park. They raced around the climbing frames and slides. Meanwhile many cars passed, carrying a multitude of family heading up to Tilly's house. The girls soon headed back for lunch.

Family and friends filled out the garden, kitchen and living room as Tilly's Nanny arrived, the air filled with chatter and long conversations. The girls went up to Tilly's room where Harley had brought around her 'Hero adventure' game.

They had set it out all over the floor completely filling the room with imaginative models, buildings and little characters

12

with no shortage of silly voices, Until...

"Tilly, can you come down, Nan wants you for just a moment," called up Tilly's mum.

"Yes, two secs!, I'll be back girls," Tilly shouted, as she dashed down and out in to the garden.

 Her Nan was sitting in a chair under the shade of the tree, she was holding and admiring a large selection of flowers.

"Ah, Matilda, my you are getting tall aren't you?" she said happily.

"Yes she is Mum, she's nearly ten as well," said Tilly's mum as she was passed

the large selection of
flowers. She placed
them down with the
collection of presents,
cards and many, many
more flowers.

"Can you put these in some water
my dear?" asked Nanny.

"Of course Mum, I'll see if I can find
a bucket...or two," She nudged Tilly's
shoulder as she passed her, "Tills don't
forget,"

"Huh? Oh yes, Happy Birthday
Nanny!" she cheered as she ran up and
hugged her, "I hope you like your
presents!"

"I do, they are very nice thank you
dear! But Matilda, I have some very

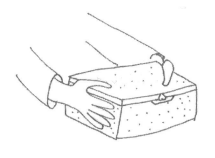

important for you today, something very special," Nanny smiled and she reached down to her large handbag, she pulled out a small very shiny silver tin.

"Shiny!" remarked Tilly.

"Yes it is," Nanny chuckled, "Now this is a very important and magical tin to me, because you see Matilda it was giving to me by my nanny when she was seventy years old and now it's time for me to pass it on, to you" she said handing it forwards.

"Wow, really, but it must be so old and if so then it's very important! Well that's what Mrs Malt says," Tilly held the tin curiously in her hands.

"Yes very old, like me" smiled Nanny, "Now this is a very magical tin, I think that you are going to enjoy what will happen. But first you must be very careful to look after this tin for me, as now it's yours Matilda, do you think you can" she explained.

Tilly nodded, "Yes I will, thank you so much Nanny I will look after it forever! Wait, what is that? What's inside?" she asked confused as she shook it, several things rustled around inside.

"Well there's only one way to find out, maybe your friends can help you investigate?" Nanny suggested as she sat back and smiled, Tilly smiled back before darting back inside and up the stairs.

"Girls look what I just got given!" Tilly barged back into her room, dropping to the floor to show off the tin, they felt the smooth silver.

"So shiny!" remarked Harley.

"What's inside, it opens here look!" said Amelia, as she found two little silver

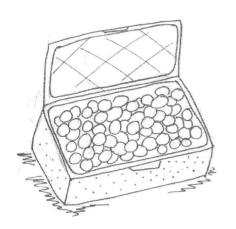

hinges on one side and a clever little silver clip on the other. She popped it and the three girls admired as they opened it to find a vast store of brightly coloured wrapped sweets.

"Wow!" they cheered happily as they each started picking out a few sweets each.

They were wrapped in brightly coloured wrappers, twisted into bows in a rainbow of colours.

"Sweets!" shouted Harley happily.

"Yes! Thank you Nanny! Shall we try one, what do you think they are?"

asked Tilly immediately unwrapping a blue one and trying it, "They are very sweet, chewy, toffee I think, go ahead, try one girls!"

The three of them each tried a delicious toffee sweet when things began to feel strange. Something almost magical seeming started to happen. It started with a bright white flash as Tilly's bedroom disappeared around them! They found themselves suddenly floating in a swirl of sparkling endless possibilities and colours!

Tilly, Harley and Amelia were about to go on the first of many amazing adventures together!

Swish! Swoop! Shwing!

Another bright flash of light and the three friends were all suddenly standing outside in a large concrete work district. Ahead of them, filling the view was a massive factory. It held massive pipes and towers. There were fantastically tall chimneys and even taller towers and offices. There were flashing lights and loud machines and horns and flags. The three stood amazed, this was definitely not Tilly's bedroom!

"What just happened?" Amelia asked, turning to the others and immediately realised that they were all dressed very differently. "What are we wearing?" she asked looking down at herself.

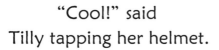

The three were all dressed in long dark blue overalls, with big pockets, name tags and white hardhats.

"Cool!" said Tilly tapping her helmet.

"Why are we dressed like builders?" asked Harley, exploring the very deep pockets, only finding bits of fluff.

Suddenly a whistle was blown and two metal doors on the factory flung open! A massive purple carpet sprung out across the concrete unrolling and creating a long purple walkway. It unfurled and ended just at the girls' feet. From the end of the rug surprisingly a man rolled out! He was dressed in similar overalls and writing on a clip board. He stepped off as the carpet ended at the three girls feet. Not looking up from his clipboard, he began to speak.

"You're late!" he tutted, "You are our new testers, this way please," he turned walking along the purple carpet at a brisk pace.

The three girls looked at one another rather bewildered by the events.

"We're testers?" Tilly questioned curiously.

"Huh?" Amelia scratched her head confused.

"Yes, yes, now please do hurry!" he continued on lifting through sheets of paper.

The girls all slowly started to follow, however stepping on to the purple carpet was only the start of bizarre! Without warning the carpet swung up, flinging the four of them all towards the factory! In a magical purple movement the carpet swung around the four of them encapsulating them all within a cylinder of purple.

"Wait…" tried Harley.

"What…" went Amelia.

"Wee" Cheered Tilly, as the cylinder began shrinking and turned from carpet to

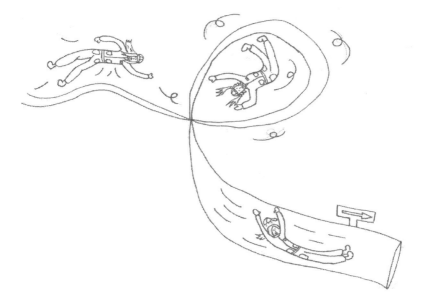

bright plastic, that they slid down like a tube slide.

"Tilly what has your Nan done to us?" asked Amelia as they slid down the slide.

"I have no idea! But it's exciting isn't it?" Cheered Tilly throwing her hands up.

"Where are we going!" called out Harley.

They didn't have long to wait as the purple slide quickly came to an end. The four of them were all spat out, landing in a pile aboard a log flume. The clipboard man stood at the front of the log as the girls sorted

themselves out. He explained that this flume would take them throughout the factory.

There were pipes and tanks of many colours! There were conveyor belts and machines everywhere. Stamping! Pressing! Squeezing and shaping! Cooking and chopping! Slicing and sorting! There were giant cranes and drones lifting and carrying, hauling and lugging. There were boxes and sacks, tubes and packets filled with a massive array of sweets; toffees and jellies, chocolates and fudges, biscuits and colourful drinks. Just about anything sweet and delicious you could imagine!

"Wow, this is amazing," Amelia gasped at the colourful machines working away.

"Look at all the sweets!" pointed Tilly, staring at the piles of delicious looking sweets.

"Wow, what's that?" asked Harley pointing an area containing a large pool of water with a sandy tropical island, with palm trees and a small pirate ship anchored off its shore.

"That is Pirate Island, where we dig up all of our gold chocolate coins" explained the man as he wrote on his clipboard.

"And what's that?" asked Amelia, pointing to a far off quarry, with miners and cranes working away.

"That would be our state of the art toffee quarry, where our masons cut only the finest slabs of toffee," he explained proudly as he shuffled paperwork.

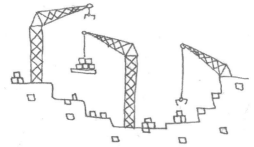 The whimsical wonder of this place had a wonderful magical feeling about it, the girls had a million and one questions about this place. But before they could ask, the log flume brought them in a room of slides, there were dozens of tubes, slides that lead to all parts of the factory.

The man with the clipboard jumped out of the log with ease.

"Testers this way," he said.

"Wait, sir, we don't even know you name yet," said Amelia as she helped Tilly out of the boat.

"Carl, I am the Head of Inspection, now hurry girls, we are on a timetable," explained Carl tapping his pen on his watch, leading them to a green slide entrance.

"What should we do?" asked Amelia.

"This is a very strange place, but it feels nice," said Harley.

"Strange yes, but I think we should go with the flow, I mean we've come this far, we can only find out more by moving forwards," Tilly put her hand forward and the three of them towered their hands before following Carl down the green tube.

Swirl! Squelch! Swish!

After a bright green curling and
whirling ride on the slide, the three came
to land in a very muddy fudge swamp,
with thick liquorice roots and trees filling
out the drippy atmosphere.

"Now this is cool!" commented
Tilly, as she started to inspect one of the
liquorice trees.

"Tilly, this is kind of spooky," said Harley as she grabbed at Amelia arm. There was a slight misty fog between the trees, and there were lots of ditches and large gaps in the fudge floor, the green water level seemed lower than your average fudge swamp.

Snap! Tilly broke off a twig from the tree and immediately began to chew, "Mmm!"

"It is nice?" asked Amelia.

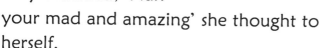

"It's really nice, it's a tree made of liquorice, that's mad!" Tilly chuckled, 'Nan your mad and amazing' she thought to herself.

The three of them grew a little more confident as they started to explore into the swamp. They walked around what had been a rather large body of water, but was now barely a puddle. Tilly spotted Carl, he was standing with his clipboard looking up to a metal pipe. A pipe which was overgrown with roots and vines all made from liquorice. He poked at it with his pen and began to tut.

Tut!   Tut!   Tut!

"Oh that doesn't look so good," pointed Amelia.

"It is not, no. The main pipe has been blocked. Now the Fizz drink isn't filling up the swamp lands, this must be opened immediately, or else Fizz production will cease to continue. And a fudge swamp without a fizzing green drink is hardly a fudge swamp at all! I will have to inform a maintenance team," explained Carl, examining his clipboard.

"So its needs opening?" Tilly asked as she began scheming and looking around.

"Well, this is only liquorice right? We need something heavy, something strong perhaps" Amelia thought aloud as she investigated the blockage. She snapped away a few lose twigs still pondering.

"Hey, Amelia," said Harley tapping her friend's shoulder.

"Hold on I'm thinking!" said Amelia scratching her chin.

"Amelia!" shouted Harley, grabbing he waist and pulling her back just in time as...

"Charge!" yelled Tilly, she charged with energetic fury across the fudge with a massive log of liquorice. Everyone jumped out of the way, as Tilly charged against the pipe. The massive log went crashing,

smashing away the massive growth of vines and roots, the overwhelming sudden force punched straight through all of the blockage.

"Yes!" cheered Tilly triumphantly.

Splash!

The pipe burst forth with a thick green fizzy drink, a massive wave blasted forth sweeping all three of the girls and washing them up in a pile on the fudge shore.

"Again!" shouted Tilly jumping up, as the others lay there in shock, now soaked and sticky.

"Harley?"

"Yes Amelia,"

"I think she's the mad one" said Harley

"Agreed, but you just have to love her!" The girls grinned at each other, "Well Carl, the pipe is now open!"

"Hm, yes indeed. Great job testers, now," he said pulling out a glass beaker, filling the beaker with the green bubbling liquid, he held it up and watched it bubble away, "Now time for a taste test!" he offered the tall beaker to Tilly.

Tilly brushed away her hair and held up the beaker, the three girls all stood in a circle watching it bubble away.

"What do you think it tastes like?" asked Harley.

"Only one way to find out," said Tilly as she took the plunge, tipping up the beaker. "Wow, it's really sweet and fizzing," The liquid continued to fizz and bubble as she passed it around and they all had a taste.

It was fizzy with a strong lime taste
to it, the girls were all filled with bubbles.
They had one last look at the swamp,
then suddenly there was a bright white
flash and the three all appeared back to
Tilly bedroom, sitting around on the floor
dressed back to normal, dry and no
longer sticky.

The girls giggled, still very filled with
bubbles and very puzzled they looked at

one another. Tilly quickly
jumped up to the
window, the party was
still happening in the
garden as she caught the
eye of her Nanny. She
gave a smile and winked
as Tilly chuckled.

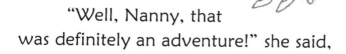

   "Well, Nanny, that
was definitely an adventure!" she said,

turning back. The three girls all started laughing.

Little did they know this was only the start of their amazing adventures together.

Extreme Fishing

Drip! Drip! Drip!

"Oh I'm so bored!" Tilly complained, as she hung over her bean  bag and looked out through the gap in the tarp cover of her den to the garden getting slowly flooded with rain.

"Well we were going to go swimming but the pool was closed," Harley explained bored.

"You might be able to swim out there in a minute, it's been raining all week!" Amelia said, looking up from her new book.

"But why did they have to be closed on the weekend! Now we have nothing to do!" Tilly grumbled.

"My Daddy said that they are installing new filters or pipes or something, but they're going to be closed for a while." Amelia explained from behind her book.

"So what are we going to do instead?" questioned Tilly as she rolled over and sat up.

"You can help me finish these new game boards," Harley said walking back to their table, she had emptied out her

craft box of
pens, paints,
glue and
colourful
decorations.

She had a
number of cut
out shapes and a variety of fun recycled
objects like cardboard, papers and
magazines to work with. Harley opened
her glue stick and starting working with
the tissues paper. Tilly rolled off of her
bean bag and lazily wandered over to
Harley. As she picked up a pair of scissors.
Then suddenly the strange silver tin, sitting
on the old bookshelf, began to glow
brightly.

"Oh look its
happening again!" Tilly

looked up in fascination.

"What?" asked Amelia looking up from her book worried, "Oh no, not again,"

Tilly quickly jumped up and grabbed the tin bringing it across to the table. "Let's see!" she started pulling back the lid to reveal the vast selection of sparking sweets.

"No, we're not going to the factory again are we?" asked Amelia.

"Well we'll see! Where is it going to take use this time? Come on and pick one girls!" Tilly

 instructed excitedly as she picked out a yellow sweet and offered the tin across.

"Only if Amelia comes," said Harley hesitantly putting her hand over the tin. The two girls looked at Amelia, Tilly shook the tin impatiently waiting for adventure.

"Oh alright then," Amelia put down her book and approached the tin, "Hopefully wherever we end up is drier than this!" she said as the two girls each picked out a yellow sweet. They unwrapped and began to eat their sweets.

A familiar feeling return. There was a sudden flash of light and the girls fell into a sparking swirl of endless possibility.

Swish! Swoop! Shwing!

There was another bright flash of light as the three girls suddenly found themselves dressed bright long yellow rain coats, long black waders and bright yellow hats and standing on the deck of ship.

"Oh no," murmured Amelia as the moment she opened her eyes a great wave rose  and splashed all of the girls in to a pile on the deck. They became immediately soaked and bright flashing lighting filled the sky. Wave after wave struck the deck of the ship, the girls had found themselves on a stormy sea adventure!

"We're on the sea!" Tilly shouted excited, grabbing a wooden hand rail and pulling herself up to see the  rolling storming waves of the ocean.

"And I was hoping it would be a dry adventure," Amelia worried, hugging Harley as the two of them held on to Tilly as the small vessel was charging up and down massive waves in an extremely powerful storm.

"All hands ready!" At this loud shout the door to the helm was thrown open as a towering tall captain stepped out on to the deck. He had a great white beard, an eye-catching eye patch and a grand captain's hat atop his head! He began to pull at a rope mounted to small crane and tossed the end of the rope to the three girls.

"Haul away crew, this storms a fierce one and we still be needing to haul in our last catch!" The Captain shouted as he started to open a metal hatch on the deck.

"What?" asked a confused Harley.

"I think he means pull it in," said Amelia clutching her arm.

"Why didn't he just say so then?" said Tilly beginning to drag the rope, the others got to their feet and all began to drag the rope. It looped around the crane and down in to the dark waves, as they dragged it got heavier and heavier the metal arm of crane was starting to bend.

"Is it meant to do that?" asked Tilly, pointing.

"Aye! Keep hauling, she's old, but we need this catch!" The Captain shouted back.

"Pull!" Commanded Tilly as the girls all pulled together. They pulled! They hauled! The rope was heavy and the storm continued to rock the ship. The ship creaked and wailed in the storm.

Suddenly thunder roared above them! Lighting flashed bright across the sky! The old metal arm of crane let out a mighty crack **And...**

Crash! Splash! Twang!

The rope and crane all whipped away and were eaten by the waves! The girls all let go of the rope as they crashed in to another pile on the deck.

"Oh Scallops!" The Captain yelled as he slammed the hatch closed on the deck and raced to the ships side. Looking down in to the depths, he paused for a moment before another giant wave crashed over onto the deck.

The Captain hurried back to the helm, passing the girls clinging to the ships side "All hands below! We're heading back to port!"

Trudging after him to the helm the girls found their way below deck to a rather cramped but comfortable cabin, they hung up their dripping yellow coats, hats and waders and all collapsed on to the bed, wrapping themselves in a fluffy blanket.

"Anyone else really worn out?" Amelia yawned.

"Very and also wet and cold!" Harley said with a shiver, as he brushed wet hair from her face.

"Tiring yes, but very exciting! The Captain said we are heading back to shore where it'll probably be much drier, but until then let's have a look around" Tilly jumped up out of the blanket. She began to curiously dig though the various cupboards and cabinets that were built into the walls of this cabin.

In these cupboards were a great variety of knickknacks and curios. There was fishing tackle, old binoculars, woolly jumpers, a compass and a vast collection of maps and nautical charts. There was gold and silver coins, there were beautiful shells and a number of long sharp teeth strung across the walls. There was an old lantern and mounted on the wall in a secure metal hoop was a glass bottle with a little model of a ship inside.

"Look at all of this, cool huh?" admired Tilly.

"Land Ho!" The Captain shouted from above.

Back up on deck, the storm had cleared up and their ship was moving into a very busy port. There was a half a dozen other vessels, sailors delivering cargo and preparing to launch, going about their business in the most busy way possible.

The Captain brought their ship into dock, the girls stood at the ship's bow watching the business unfold. The Captain opened the ships hatch and allowed men from the docks to unload a rather poor catch of fish and move them towards carts parked along the busy front.

Unfortunately the Captain was paid quite little for his catch, the much larger ship across from them had a vast selection of eyes looking upon, then laughing at their catch.

"Bout' time to call it quits old man!"

"Look at that catch, how lousy!"

"Hey Gramps, is that what's left of your crew? Hah!"

They laughed on but the Captain stood strong ignoring their bullying words standing atop the deck as the girls walked alongside him.

"Well that wasn't very kind," Harley stated crossing her arms.

"No but they are right, I'm far too old for this game," the Captain sighed as he sat on a barrel, pulling off his hat.

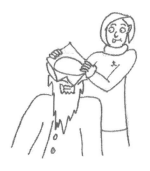

"Don't say that Captain! Don't let them tell you what you can and can't do! Your catch got away this time, but it's not the end" Encouraged Tilly as she picked up his hat and planted it atop his head rather crooked.

"No?" asked the Captain.

"Not while we're still here, right," said Tilly, as the three girls joined hands with the Captain encouragingly.

"Right!" added Harley.

"We're going to prove those bullies wrong! But what are we going to do about a new catch?" asked Amelia.

The captain scratched his white beard thoughtfully for a moment. A smile grew across his salty aged face before he stood up adjusting his hat. "I have an idea," He announced, the girls cheered!

So together they all set back out to the open sea, back to the rolling waters but this time with clear skies, a repaired boat and renewed determination and optimism. The port was soon far from view as they approached a new location at the Captain's orders. They were near a mass of cliffs, atop which a lighthouse stood tall and proud with its red and

white striped tower and beaming lantern.

Now the Captain, long in beard and strong in mind announced his idea. However his plan may have needed a little more thinking through!

"Wait, what? You need this much bait?!" exclaimed Amelia.

"Aye, we be needing all the bait we have," announced the Captain, as he set to work, he laid ropes 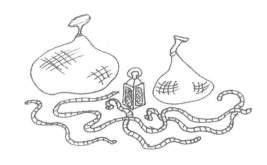 along the deck and unpacked a selection of nets full of bait.

"So we'll be catching a fish with all this bait? A single fish?" questioned Tilly.

"She be much more than a wee fish lassie!" explained the Captain, standing and looking out at the ocean, "A Sparkling Rainbow Trout, a living legend to all us Sailors! Many Captains on many vessels have attempted to catch such massive beauties!"

"So it's a big fish?" added Tilly sarcastically, crossing her arms.

"If it's such a legend, how can you be sure it even exists?" questioned Amelia, piling on more bait.

"I know because I has seen one with my very own eye! It had passed through my nets many times, always by these cliffs and shores, but I've never been able to scoop it fast enough. But not today! If I'm going to prove my worth as the Captain then the Sparkling Rainbow Trout is the best way! Now my crew are ye ready to help me?" The Captain turned to his three deckhands.

The three girls looked at each other before nodding confidently to one another, "We're in, what do you need?" asked Tilly.

"We'll be needing all of this here bait girls but also we'll have to pull out all the stops. Green lights to attract the trout to your location. Now who here can swim?" Asked the Captain with a chuckle as he held up a glowing green lantern.

Tilly and Amelia looked at one another, they both looked worried, Amelia fiddling with her thumbs. They turned towards Harley blinking as she moved with speed to the side of the boat.

"What?" She questioned with a raised eyebrow, as in a flash she was already standing on a plank hanging over

 the waves. The Captain had tied a rope to her middle and she was dressed ready to swim with flippers and goggles!

"Hey, how come I'm the only one standing here! Come on Amelia and Tilly you're both better swimmers then me and Tilly you're the one that even wanted to go swimming today!" Harley pointed out.

"Well I can't get my arm wet with sea water, the salt will cause problems!" explained Amelia.

"Yes and besides, I'm here with the Captain to pull up nets! And Harley you always say you can hold breath longer than us and you're much braver than us and you really like fish!" Tilly bumbled through multiple reasons, trying to not look at the depths of the calm blue ocean.

"Ok fine, I'll do this part then!" said Harley rolling her eyes at her friends but smiling as she accepted the lantern.

"Don't worry there matey, we have your line nice and secure. We'll soon pull you up if there's danger!" said the Captain as he adjusted his Captain's hat.

Harley looked down at the water as she clutched the lantern, it was glowing bright green. For a moment, her legs shook a bit more than she wanted so she took a moment to breathe and think. 'I must be crazy, but here we go' she thought to herself. She took in a deep breath and dove in to the water.

Splash! It wasn't as cold as it looked. As Harley slowly swam down, she looked at the underside of the ship, it was covered in barnacles and bits of coral spiralling in lots of

68

different colours. The waters were calm, as the endless blue void carried off in all directions with light seeping in and out rather beautifully. Directly below she could just make out the rocky sea floor, with little worlds of coral and sand. There was a grand selection of fish all wondering

who this new visitor was. Harley turned and swam down a little more, she held out the lamp as the green glow carried out across the void. The net plunged above holding tons of fish bait, hoping for the light to attract their specific legendary catch.

'I wonder if this lantern will actually work?' Harley wondered as she shone it in different directions.

She turned around again, there was still nothing, 'Come on fishy,' she thought. Still no major movements so she swam back to the surface, breaking the waves with a gasp.

"Are you alright Harls?" called Tilly.

"Yeah, no sign of the fish yet!" Harley called, "Going back down again!"

She took another deep breath and dove back down.

She swam straight down towards the sea floor, she landed on a area of sand and held up the lamp, 'Come on fishy, we haven't all day,' she thought.

Only something was different, she turned around, all of the fish had disappeared, 'That's odd' she though, she turned around again. There she spotted a very tiny fish swimming towards her, 'Ah there's one, a nice little one' she thought, only as it got closer did she realize that

71

it wasn't a little fish. It was a massive fish! With bright shiny scales, long fins and a hungry look. And it was swimming straight towards her.

'Oh no, not nice, not nice fishy!' Harley realised as tugged hurriedly at her rope and quickly scrammed back towards the ship, Harley was thankfully fished from the water in seconds.

Splash!
Crash!
Ahh!

Harley crashed on to the deck. Only the massive fish followed. It burst up through the water, breaking the initial baited net, flying up and jumping over the ship. It's scales shone brightly, rainbows sparkling across the deck, the girls watched in awe. It dove back towards the water just as the Captain cast a second

massive net. It wrapped around the trout as it dove in to the water. The ropes pulled slack and pulleys strained as the massive creature moved quick dragging the ropes and ship all towards the cliff side.

"She's pulling us, quickly, we need to reel her in before she grounds us on the cliff!" Shouted the Captain, as he tossed ropes to girls.

Everyone heaved and hauled with all their strength as the ship was dragged faster and faster.

"Pull!" shouted Tilly

"Heave!" called Amelia

"Nearly there mates!" shouted the captain.

An almighty effort from everyone followed by the biggest splash ever, saw the giant fish lifted and crashing down on to the deck just in time! The Captain quickly veered the ship away from the rocky shores, the girls all collapsed into an exhausted pile.

"Phew," they all went at a job well done.

Never were there some many dropped jaws as they returned to the port with the massive Sparkling Rainbow Trout suspended above their ships deck! Every sailor, captain and dock worker clapped, cheered, looking on with amazement. The Captain heaved his catch on to the dockside, he stood proud as the girls all stood holding hands on the side of the ship.

"Well that was easy huh?" said Tilly beaming.

"For you, maybe" Harley laughed as she elbowed Tilly. She pushed her back a bit, and before long the girls were being silly and playful. With one wrong move combined with the rocking of the Captain's ship Tilly tumbled over the side towards the water. But before the others could laugh, she grabbed both of their coats and the three of them all tipped, tumbled and crashed into the water.

Crash!

Splash!   Flash!

A sudden white light glowed as the three girls returned to their den, all of them completely soaked as the storm continued to hammer down outside. The three of them all started laughing as they cleared the wet hair from their eyes.

"Girls, you better come back inside I don't want you sailing away out there!" Shouted Tilly's mum from the back door.

The three of them laughed together before rushing back in to the warm to dry off after their adventure on the grand open ocean aboard the Captain's Ship!

Little Garden Helpers

"Girls! Look its glowing again!" Tilly rushed out from the garden den to where Amelia and Harley were relaxing in the shade under the fence. Tilly clutched the magical silver tin, it shone with a bright glow as Tilly lifted the lid. "Shall we see what's going to happen this time?"

Amelia and Harley looked at one another.

"Well, I hope it's not going to be cold," Amelia said as she picked out one.

"And I'm not being bait again!" Harley stated.

The girls picked out some pink sparkling sweets. As they chewed on the delicious toffee treat, lights flashed and they returned to the now familiar glowing and sparkling light of possibilities.

Swish!

Swoop! Shwing!

82

Another bright flash followed and they looked around. Their outfits had not changed, it was still a beautiful sunny afternoon in the garden. But then they noticed the tall garden fence was taller than before! The girls had shrunk, no taller than blades of grass now surrounding them. The garden was now an endless maze of grass.

"Well, at least we're not cold. But Tilly, you and Harley are tiny!" sad Amelia

"No need to be rude Amelia, just cause you're the tallest! I'm sure we'll have growth spurts soon, maybe we'll be as tall as the tree!" Tilly laughed as she helped Harley to climb up the blade of grass.

"Wow look at that!" Harley gasped, lying on the grass looking like a mountain range in the distance was a packet of chewy sweets.

They must have fallen out of her pocket before their adventure.

"Now that is a big bag of sweets!" Tilly laughed.

Twinkle! Twinkle!

"What was that?" asked Amelia curious as Harley and Tilly were entranced by the size of the sweets.

"What was what?" Tilly looked up confused.

"Didn't you here the noise, like, like a something strange, you know I'm not sure" Amelia balanced on the blade of grass cupping her ears for the sound.

Twinkle! Twinkle!

"There you must have heard it that time!" Amelia gestured as she stood next to the girls. They were no longer focused on the sweets and looked out at the sea of grass curious about this unknown sound. Harley grabbed Tilly as she curiously looked around.

Twinkle!

Twinkle! Swoosh!

There was a sudden movement through the blades of grass. The girls leaned and stared, then suddenly they spotted two little eyes staring back at them.

"Ah!" They jumped back startled and slipping off of their perch on the blade of grass. The girls fell off and landed in a pile on the mud!

Oof!

Ow!

Crunch!

"On no, I'm so sorry, I didn't mean to make you jump," A soft voice called out to them. There was a flicker of light and a rain of sparkling gold dust erupted as a fairy floated towards the pile of girls.

Tilly, Amelia and Harley all stared in amazement from the mud.

"Are you ok?" She asked as she helped up them to their feet.

"We're fine! Oh my! You're a fairy?" asked Tilly.

"A real fairy?" asked Harley excitedly.

"Very convincing if not," added Amelia examining the fluttering wings.

"I am in fact a fairy!" She giggled, "I'm Lily a garden fairy, a fairy at your service!" She fluttered about around the girls excitedly, gold fairy dust flying off of

her sparkling wings, catching on the girls'
clothes.

"Oh whoops sorry," chuckled Lily,
dusting some of the dust off of Tilly's
head. Amelia
sneezed from the
dust catching her
nose.

"No
worries," Laughed
Tilly as she walked
around Lily
looking at her
wings. They
sparkled and flapped softly in the air.
They held delicate details which caught
the light in beautiful ways.

"What do garden fairies do Lily?"
asked Amelia curiously.

"Well, I'm a garden guardian! I help look after this garden throughout the seasons," Lily smiled, "What are you girls doing down here. I mean this is your garden but you're normally much bigger, what happened?"

"Well that's a story and 'alf, but today we're on a adventure," explained Tilly.

"A Magical Adventure," added Harley.

"Wow, well I hope you enjoy your adventure in the garden. Personally I am very pleased with my work, this is the first garden I'm looking after on my own and there lots to do so it keeps me very occupied," explained Lily.

"Oh, well yes, it's a very nice garden, but that sounds very lonely," Tilly thought as she looked at the girls before an idea struck her, "Maybe we can help you today?"

"Really?" asked Lily, her eyes lighting up brighter.

"Yes, that's what friends are for," said Amelia hooking arms with Harley.

"Right, and when your jobs are finished we can all play together if you want," added Harley.

"Play, really, I've never had the time to play, there's always so much to do," explained Lily pulling out a leaf list.

"Well we'd better get the work finished, what do we have to do today?" asked Tilly.

Lily scratched her nose and began to examine her list.

She clicked her fingers excitedly and reached into her little brown satchel. She pulled out a handful of green and orange dust, "I've got to help the ants begin their new colony, but it's a long way and flying is always the best way to travel!" Lily explained before throwing the sparkling dust over the girls.

"Flying?" asked Harley, brushing the dust out of her eyes only to notice that

they were starting
to float above the
ground.

"Hold on,"
Lily laughed as she
took Tilly's hand
and began to fly up. Amelia and Harley
grabbed on to Tilly's legs as they all flew
high into the air above the sea of grass
and began to zoom across the garden.

The four of them flew through the
air, leaving a sparkling trail!

"Wow this is amazing!" shouted
Tilly, "Amelia, Harley, we're really
flying!"

"I know, Harley open your eyes!"
called out Amelia to Harley, who face was
all scrunched up,

"Ok," she said slowly taking a peep, as they passed over a small group of dandelions. Harley smiled and then started to laugh, "Yay!" she cheered.

All the others cheered as Lily lead them through the air. She darted gracefully in and out and around the really tall blades of grass, as they headed towards the base of the now giant tree. Time to being Lily's long list of work!

They all started at the new ant hill, there were thousands of ants moving into their new tunnels. Lily was sure to check that they were settling in, that the tunnels were tidy and they had plenty of space. Tilly, Harley and Amelia tried moving some food for the ants but didn't have nearly the same amount of strength as the ants!

Next they had to fly high, high up in
to the tree. Here among the branches and
leaves, a massive collection of bees where
working in their golden hive. Lily
introduced the girls to the great queen
bee, the regal leader of the hive. Together
they enjoyed a polite afternoon tea with
the freshest honey on tiny fairy scones.
This job, taste-testing the honey was Lily's
favourite task. It was now also Tilly's
favourite job!

Then on a higher branch of the tree, Tilly, Harley and Amelia helped a family of magpies to build an addition to their nest so that mum could keep her eggs safe. They had to collect lots of twigs and small stones and weave and wrap everything together. Lily helped mama magpie safely move the eggs into the new nest!

After that, Lily flew them over to the flowerbed near to the fence. The flowerbed held a variety of colourful and beautifully blooming flowers. The flowers were all growing high and healthy, but a few were crooked and falling. The girls all worked hard together to make sure that they were all based in the ground and standing straight and tall so they could see the sun and making sure they were properly watered.

It was a long and busy afternoon,
but after working hard together, Lily had
completed her long list of garden guardian
jobs. They had plenty of time left over to
play. The girls all raced in and out of
grass, they chased and charged. They
played hide and
seek. Amelia
made a little
flying disk out a
leaf as they
tossed it from
one another,

playing catch when you can fly it just the
best way to play. They laughed and
cheered as Lily absolutely beamed with
happiness and cheer, golden dust spiralling
from her wings.

It was starting to get late so after one last flight across the garden, the four of them all came to sit along the garden wall and look back at all of their hard work. It had been a very long afternoon and it was starting to get dark.

"I'm so very tired now," Grumbled Tilly as she leaned on Amelia.

"You've all been ever so helpful, I don't know if I would have gotten everything done today without your help and this was so very much fun!" said Lily gratefully.

"Well it's not every day we meet a fairy, this was awesome Lily," said Amelia.

"I'm going to miss you girls," said Lily as she pulled the three of them all into a hug. Her wings flapped as gold dust covered them and in a flash of gold and white light, the girls opened their eyes. They were back in the garden, in the shade, back to their regular sized selves.

Brushing gold dust from their eyes they stood up and looked up in to the tree. They saw the nest and the hive, they saw the lovely flowers and all of the little creatures crawling along under the grass.

"Wow, what an adventure in our very own garden." said Harley, "Do you think we'll meet Lily again?"

"Maybe," said Tilly as she hugged their silver tin.

"I hope so, but let's go in, it's getting cold out here." shivered Amelia, heading towards the back door, Harley followed as Tilly took one last look around the base of tree.

Just for a moment in the corner of her eyes she saw something, maybe something, a flicker, a sparkle, a twinkle, or was it just the light, who could say?

Twinkle!

Twinkle!

Twinkle!

Medieval Meddling

Ding!
Ding!
Ding!

"Phew it's been a long day!" sighed Harley as she walked down the stairs and through the busy hallway.

"Wait for me Harley!" called Tilly as she pushed through the bustling crowds of students.

They joined together with their coats done up and backpacks over their shoulders. They walked down the hall, through the green doors and out on to the playground.

"There they are," said Tilly, pointing out their mums' standing by the blue fence. Tilly's younger brother was already with them and Harley's little sister was waving from the pram. The girls walked across ready for home time.

"Whatever are we going to do for our home learning this time?" asked Harley.

"Hmmm, what if we, um, or, perhaps, maybe Amelia can help. Mummy?" asked Tilly, "When is Amelia going to be home?"

"I'm not sure, she went to the Doctors, so she might be back late," Mum explained.

Tilly dropped her bag in the hallway and kicked off her shoes.

After rooting around in her school bag she pulled out her textbook. She and Harley took their books into the front room. They sat and Tilly poured a box of pens, paints and brushes all over the carpet.

"Have you got any ideas Tilly?" asked Harley.

"Well, if we get stuck, Daddy said we could use his computer, but I think I have a better idea," explained Tilly

The doorbell rang. Tilly's mum answered to Amelia and her mum.

"Girls! Amelia's here!" Tilly's mum called as she invited Amelia's Mum into the kitchen for a cup of tea.

"Hello!" called Amelia bouncing into the front room with a big smile. She couldn't wait to show the girls her arm. Amelia's prosthetic arm had to be adjusted today to keep up with Amelia as she grows.

"Wow!" went Harley.

"I love the new patterns," Tilly said

"Cool, isn't it, watch this," Amelia showed it off to the girls. They sat in a circle and shared their home learning project with Amelia.

"So, we have to find out an interesting fact about Medieval times. Then Miss will take them all, put them altogether and as a class we will build a large poster," explained Harley.

"Do you have any ideas yet?" asked Amelia.

"Well..." Harley began.

"Yes, I know just what to do," Interrupted Tilly, as she jumped up and ran out of the room. "Come on girls, follow me!" she called, as she lead them to the den in the garden.

Inside the den on the little table was their mysterious silver tin.

"Oh no! Till, you're not going to try these again are you? We'll be sucked into another wacky and wild adventure," warned Amelia.

"It'll be fine, and it'll be fun!" said Tilly confidently as the three of them stood around the silver tin. Tilly unclipped the latch, pulling back the lid to reveal a collection of bright sparkling wrappers of sweets.

"Let's try a blue one," she said, as they all picked out one, unwrapped it and began chewing. Amelia plugged her ear and 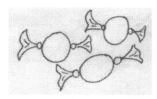 Harley closed her eyes. There was a sudden flash of light as the girls fell into a sparkling swirl of endless possibility.

Swish!

Swoop!

Shwing!

111

Another flash of light and the three girls all stood in a forest and they were dressed very differently.

"You two are dressed very funny," giggled Tilly pointing.

"So are you!" pointed out Amelia.

Clang!

Clang!

Clang!

A sudden noise rang out over the tress.

"What was that? A bell?" Amelia wondered.

"Let's find out!" Tilly said confidently leading them through the tress.

They quickly discovered the source of the noise, and a great many other sounds. Music, chatter, laughter and joy filled the air. Medieval people were exploring a very colourful medieval fair.

There were bright colourful tents and long strings of bunting between tall wooden posts.

Everything was decorated with different blooming flowers. There was music and performers with crowds of people cheering and clapping.

"Wow, this is amazing!" exclaimed Amelia.

"Look over there, it's a castle!" Harley pointed across the fairground towards a giant stone castle with tall towers and blue pointed turrets. Bright flags waved in the wind.

In front of the castle there was a large wooden structure, with even more coloured flags and tents.

"Let's check it out! Dressed like this we can easily blend in," schemed Tilly.

"Oh, I'm not sure," Worried Harley.

"Come on, let's give it a try," said Amelia, holding Harley's hand.

Plucking up the courage the three girls walked into the giant construct. They were greeted by great cheers and shouts as

loud crashes gave view to the grand
knights dressed head to food in armour,
clashing weapons for entertainment!

Lots of people cheered and clapped.

The girls walked around a fenced
sandy battle ground just as a trumpet
sounded. The crowds clapped as the

knights halted their battles and began clearing the grounds as the next competition was about to begin.

This time the knights were leading horses and holding long wooden jousts. They charged down the grounds, attempting to knock the other off of their horse.

"Ouch, that has got to hurt!" winced Tilly.

"Can we go now?" asked Harley worried, grasping Amelia's arm.

"In a minute, what's behind there do you think?" questioned Tilly pointing across to a tent opening. Curiosity took over as the three girls passed through the tent flaps. Inside was chaos, knights and pages rushed about preparing armour and weaponry.

Stable boys rushed horses out to the grounds and nurse tended to minor injuries. The girls were very quickly swept up into the madness. Amelia was pushed back and bumped into a tall pile of carefully balanced maces.

"Whoops!" she said grabbing at one as the rest fell like dominos. Several maces crashed down on top of an unexpecting knight.

Crash!

Smash!

Bash!

"Ow," he shouted jumping up red faced with anger, steam pouring from his ears!

"Who did that? You!" he shouted pointing at Amelia. "Do you dare challenge me, the Bone Breaker,

champion of the
western plains!" he
bellowed.

Amelia was
frozen with fear, just
as Tilly pushed
forward and stared
up at the knight.
"Oh yes, we could take you any day, you
don't scare us," said Tilly pointing and
poking.

"Five rings to the victor then," said
the Bone Breaker with a big grin and
putting out his hand.

"I don't know what that is, but
challenge accepted," said Tilly confidently
shaking his hand. Before they knew it, the
girls were outside on the grounds.

Tilly had Amelia on her shoulders wearing one large suit of armour between them. Harley held the tall joust as a stable boy brought them a horse.

"Oh Tilly, how do we get into these situations?" asked Amelia as they climbed onto the horse.

"Well, I guess I have a sweet tooth and taste for adventure. Anyway we can do this!" Encouraged Tilly.

"I don't know what we even have to do!" said Amelia.

"Do you know what they have to do?" asked Harley timidly to the stable boy.

"Aye miss, ye catch five of those rings there. Knock off the challenger with this here joust and you shall win the challenge! Bone Breaker's never lost though! Good luck lasses!" Explained the boy gesturing to a selection 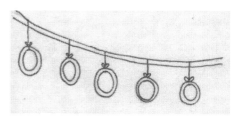 of metal rings hanging from ribbons over the length of the grounds.

"Good luck girls," said Harley passing up the joust.

"Well, at least I can test out this new arm," said Amelia lifting and locking the joust under her armoured arm and pulling down her helmet.

"Is it heavy?" asked Tilly, as the horse began to move forwards.

"Not really, this arm's a lot stronger than my old one, but I doubt Dr Spark designed it for jousting," said Amelia laughing.

Lined up and ready, there came a deep laugh from the Bone Breaker on the far side of the grounds.

"Prepare to be defeated little girls!" he shouted. They were all ready as a flag was thrown and a great cheer rose up as the horse took off!

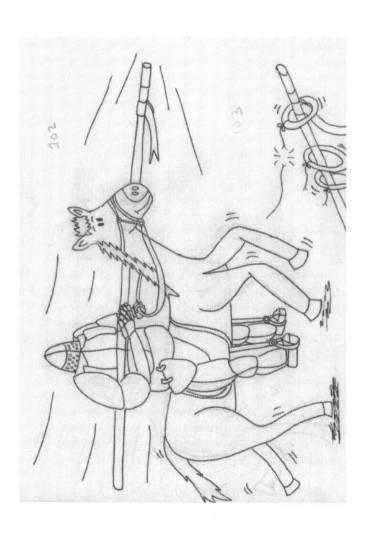

124

"Wow!" The girls charged, Amelia lifted up the joust. She caught a ring, breaking it from the ribbons. "Yes!" she cheered and then a second, "This isn't that difficult"

"Look Out!" shouted Tilly, the girls had to lean quickly as 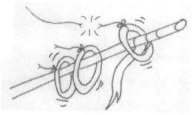 the Bone Breaker raced past fast, his joust scratching against their suit of armour.

He had already collected his five rings! The girls had missed the others are they reached the other end of the stadium. So both horses and riders lined up again for their next charge.

"That was very close," Panted Amelia.

"How we doing up there?" Tilly asked from inside the suit. However there was no time to answer as the horses charged again! "Go!" shouted Amelia as they took off again.

Both horses charged and the Bone Breaker lined up his joust for a perfect hit. However Tilly was quick to act, throwing Amelia off of her shoulders and into the air, dodging the joust and catching the last rings in a single graceful movement.

"Yes!" Laughed Amelia landing back on to Tilly's shoulders

"What!" Cried out the Bone Breaker, so distracted by the miss he didn't realise he was approaching the end of the track. His horse grinded to a stop as he was thrown into the wooden wall.

Crash!

Smash!

Ouch!

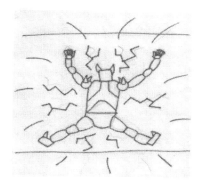

The crowds cheered as the girls climbed down from the horse as Harley joined them.

"Well done!" she cheered.

The crowds let out roaring cheers and claps as the air filled with confetti and colourful streamers.

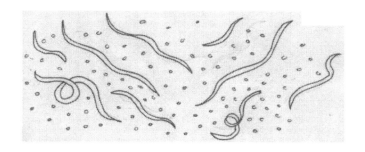

"Wow!" They all cheered. Suddenly the girls were surrounded with bright colours. In a bright flash of light they all suddenly fell back into the den, laughing as they tumbled into the pillows. They sat up, all with ribbons and confetti in their hair.

"Phew, that was fun!" said Amelia as they all laughed.

"Yes and I have an idea for class," schemed Tilly with a grin.

The following day in class, the three girls delivered their home learning all together to Mrs Malt and she and the rest of the class were very impressed with their entire presentation.

The cardboard armour was mum's good idea, a lot less heavy then real armour.

Printed by Amazon Italia Logistica S.r.l.
Torrazza Piemonte (TO), Italy

43650359R00075